P9-DDM-393

Rabbids Invasion

LAUGH YOUR RABBIDS OFF!

by Rebecca McCarthy
illustrated by Fernando Ruiz

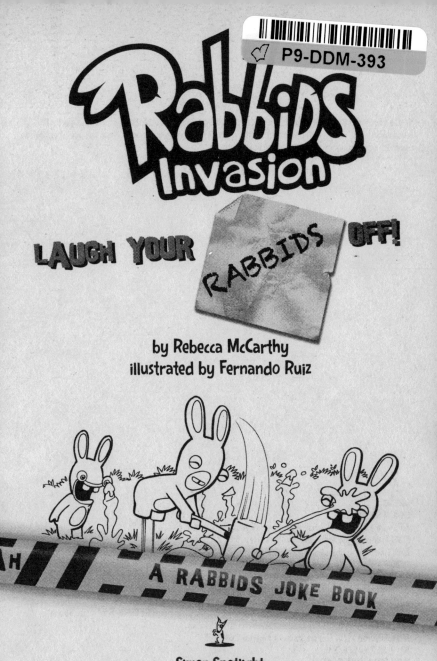

A RABBIDS JOKE BOOK

Simon Spotlight
New York London Toronto Sydney New Delhi

If you purchased this book without a cover, you should be aware that this book is stolen property. It was reported as "unsold and destroyed" to the publisher, and neither the author nor the publisher has received any payment for this "stripped book."

SIMON SPOTLIGHT

An imprint of Simon & Schuster Children's Publishing Division

1230 Avenue of the Americas, New York, New York 10020

First Simon Spotlight edition July 2014

© 2014 Ubisoft Entertainment. All rights reserved. Rabbids, Ubisoft, and the Ubisoft logo are trademarks of Ubisoft Entertainment in the U.S. and/or other countries.

All rights reserved, including the right of reproduction in whole or in part in any form.

SIMON SPOTLIGHT and colophon are registered trademarks of Simon & Schuster, Inc.

For information about special discounts for bulk purchases, please contact Simon & Schuster Special Sales at 1-866-506-1949 or business@simonandschuster.com.

Manufactured in the United States of America 0614 OFF

10 9 8 7 6 5 4 3 2

ISBN 978-1-4814-0040-4

ISBN 978-1-4814-0041-1 (eBook)

Hold on to your plungers. . . . Hide your toilet brushes. . . . Because the Rabbids are coming . . . and

THEY'RE INVADING THIS JOKE BOOK!

The Rabbids have already started to invade the planet we humans call home. That sounds *bwahfully serious, right?* But Rabbids are more likely to make you laugh till snot comes out your nose than make you quake in your boots. So prepare to stand by and guffaw as they invade the funny farm, the gym class jokes, and even the potty humor pages! But consider yourself warned: The Rabbids are bringing the funny with them, so you're in for a bwah-ha-hilarious time. . . .

What do you call a sleeping bull?

A bull dozer!

Which side of a chicken has more feathers?

The outside!

Why did the cowboy ride a horse to town?

Because it was too heavy to carry!

What did the chicken think of its new baby chick?

It was eggs-cellent.

PLAYING WITH FOOD!!!
The Rabbids don't eat. so they think food is weird.
What's it all for, anyway?

Why did the boy throw a stick of butter out the window?

Because he wanted to see a butterfly!

What is the Rabbids' favorite vegetable?

Bwahccoli

What would a Rabbid call cooking on a grill?
Bwahrbecue!

RHYME TIME:

How do you remove a mozzarella stick that's stuck up your nose?
With a cheese sneeze!

How do you make a milk shake?

You scare it!

What's the best thing to put into a pie?

Your teeth!

What happened to the girl who ate too many cookies?

She woke up feeling crummy!

What do you give to a sick lemon?

Lemon aid!

VERY RABBID RECIPES

Belgian *Bwahffles*

Whack-a-mole Guacamole

EVEN RABBIDS ~~JOKE BOOKS~~ GO TO THE POTTY

Some Rabbids broke into the police station and stole all the toilets. What happened next?

The police are investigating, but for now, they have nothing to go on!

What do you call someone who never farts in public?

A private tutor!

Knock-knock!

Who's there?

Smell mop.

Smell mop who?

No way. That's gross!

There are two reasons you should never bathe in the toilet.

Number one and number two.

What do you call it when the queen finishes up in the bathroom?

A royal flush!

Why did the boy eat a lightbulb?

He wanted a light lunch!

Why did the girl bury the flashlight?

Because the batteries died!

Why did the boy throw a grandfather clock out the window?

He wanted to see time fly.

How do you know if your clock is crazy?

It goes "cuckoo!"

Why do mice like to mop?

They want to be squeaky clean!

THE RABBIDS
GET SCHOOLED

Why did the boy eat his homework?

Because the teacher said it would be a piece of cake!

Why did the boy have a headache after school?

His teacher told him to hit the books.

Why do math tests make some kids unhappy?

Because they always have lots of problems.

What did the pen say to the pencil?

So what's your point?

Why did the boy apply for a job at the bakery?

Because he wanted to loaf around!

What kind of nails should construction workers never use to build a house?

Fingernails!

What did the cobbler say to the last customers of the day?
Shoe!

What kind of button can't be bought from a tailor?
A belly button!

Why did the waitress think the cook was mean?

Because he beat the eggs and whipped the cream.

RHYME TIME:

What do you call an ace detective?

A super snooper!

What does the doctor say to eat when you're sick?

Chicken *bwahth*

When do you usually go to the dentist?

Two thirty.

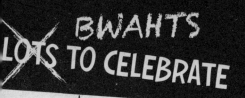

What would a Rabbid say on Christmas?

Happy *Bwahlidays!*

Did you hear about the boy who left the birthday celebration to run to the bathroom?

He was a party pooper!

Why did the football coach leave the game to go the bank?

He wanted his quarter back!

Which animals are the best baseball players?

Bats, of course! Even the Rabbids know that!

CRACK!

Why is tennis a noisy game?
Because each player raises a racket!

Why do golfers carry an extra pair of socks?
In case they get a hole in one!

BWAHAHAHA!!

What would a Rabbid call shooting hoops?
Basketbwah!

What do Rabbids use as soccer balls?
Wait . . . you mean you need soccer balls to play soccer?

What did the Rabbid say at the end of the show?

"Bwah-vo!"

Why did the duck run off stage?

He quacked under pressure.

Why did the opera singer stand on the ladder?

Because she wanted to reach the high notes!

BWAH-BWAH-BWAH BOOGIE TIME!

How do you make a tissue dance?

Put a little boogie in it!

What would a Rabbid think a trumpet is made out of?

Bwahnze

Why did the boy bang his head on the piano?

He was playing by ear!

Why are pianos hard to open?

Because the keys are inside!

RABBIDS ON THE ROAD!

What is the sleepiest part of a bus?

The wheels . . . because they are always tired.

Where do bees catch the bus?

At the buzz stop.

What do you call a helicopter with a skunk as a pilot?

A smellycopter!

What happens when a frog's car breaks down?

It gets toad away.

What kinds of snakes love cars?

Windshield vipers.

What did the traffic light say to the car?

Don't look—I'm changing!

INVADING JOKES FROM AROUND THE WORLD

Why did the Rabbid go to South America?

He wanted to visit *Bwahzil*.

Where in the world . . . do people wander around aimlessly?

Rome!

Where in the world ... do people slip and fall?

Greece!

Why did the Rabbids bring glue to the Louvre Museum?

Their tour guide told them to stick together!

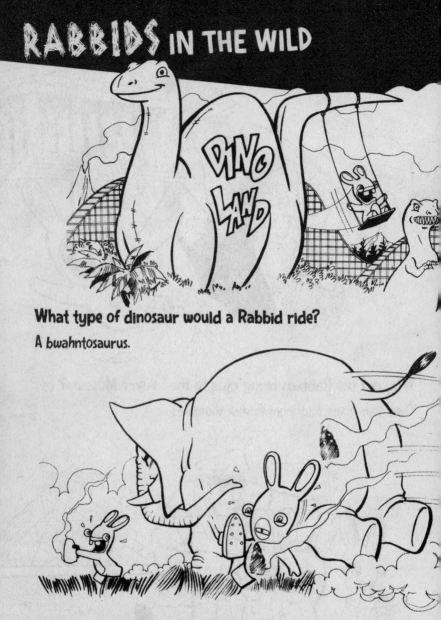

What type of dinosaur would a Rabbid ride?

A *bwahntosaurus.*

Why do elephants have wrinkles?

Ever tried to iron an elephant?

What do you call an alligator detective?
An investigator!

How do you play leapfrog with a porcupine?
Very carefully!

What's the best way to catch a fish?
Have someone throw it at you!

RABBIDS, RABBIDS, ~~WATER, WATER,~~ EVERYWHERE

Why was the ocean friendly?

Because it waved!

What kind of paper can you color on at the beach?

Sandpaper!

Why did the Rabbid get sunburned?

He forgot to apply his *bwahnzer* and sunscreen.

How do humans call their friends at the beach?

On their shell phones!

RHYME TIME:

What kind of sweets are eaten at the beach?

Sandy candy!

NAME THAT KID ... RABBIDS STYLE!

Can you help the Rabbids name the kid based on the picture?

Peg

John

Doug

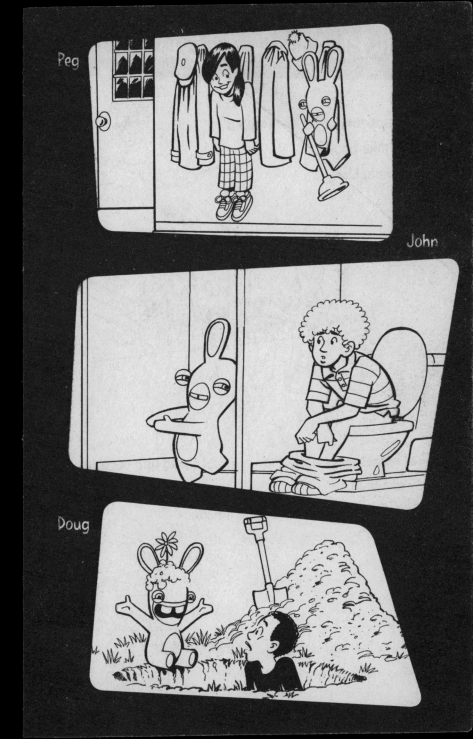

**What happened after the Rabbid
ate this joke book?**
He felt pretty funny!

**What makes more noise than a Rabbid laughing outside
your window?**
Seven Rabbids laughing outside your window!

What has two legs and says. "AHAHAAHAWB!"?
A Rabbid walking backward!

KID: Knock, knock!
DAD: Who's there?
KID: Interrupting Rabbid.
DAD: Interrupting Rab—
RABBID: BWAAAH-HA-HA!!

RABBID 1: Bwah, bwah!
RABBID 2: Bwaah bwaah?
RABBID 1: Bwah-ha-bwah-ha Rabbid.
RABBID 2: Bwah-ha-bwa—
RABBID 3: BWAAAH-HA-HA!!

Time to say bwah-bye, folks! Hope you had a Rabbid good time.

The Rabbids sure did!

Where—or what—will they invade next?
Bwahtch out, world. Here come the Rabbids!